To my mom, Joan Mulhearn, who taught me the
love of books and the joy of storytelling
—A. M. M. S.

Caps for Sale and the Mindful Monkeys
By Esphyr Slobodkina and Ann Marie Mulhearn Sayer
Production assistant & colorist Katherine Grace Larsen
Text copyright © 2017 by Ann Marie Mulhearn Sayer
Artwork copyright © 2017 by Ann Marie Mulhearn Sayer and Esphyr Slobodkina

ISBN 978-0-06-249988-2

17 18 19 20 21 SCP 10 9 8 7 6 5 4 3 2 1
❖
First Edition

CAPS FOR SALE
and the
Mindful
Monkeys

Esphyr Slobodkina

and

Ann Marie Mulhearn Sayer

HARPER
An Imprint of HarperCollinsPublishers

Pezzo the peddler sold caps.
But he was not like
an ordinary peddler,
carrying his wares on his back.
He carried them
on top of his head.

Every day,
he walked through the streets of the town,
calling, "Caps!
Caps for sale!
Fifty cents a cap!"

Every night
he sat on his bench in his yard,
making caps—
caps to sell—
fifty cents a cap.

The peddler had always enjoyed his quiet life.
But suddenly things had changed.

Now, in the big tree
in his backyard,
were sixteen monkeys.

They had followed the peddler
for two days.
And for two nights
they had slept in his tree.

This morning,
the monkeys were still there.

"You monkeys, you,"
the peddler said, shaking his finger at them.
"You must go home!"

But the monkeys
only shook their fingers
back at him and said,
"Tsz, tsz, tsz!"

Today the peddler
was going to visit his friend Essie.

Essie was wise.
She would know what to do about the monkeys.

The peddler started up the dirt road.
The monkeys started up the dirt road, too.

Right foot, left foot.
Right foot, left foot.
All in step.

When the peddler reached Essie's porch,
he pulled on the bell chain
outside her door.
The sound of the bell startled the monkeys,
and they scattered.

"Greetings, my friend," Essie said
as the peddler hurried past.

"No time for greetings," the peddler wailed.
"I am in trouble.
I need help.
I am being followed
by sixteen monkeys
WHO WILL NOT GO HOME!"

Essie was an artist.

Pointing to a chair with her paintbrush,

she said calmly,

"Sit down

and tell me what is happening."

Essie painted while she listened.

As the peddler recounted his story,

his temper rose again.

"I told them to go home.

The monkeys MUST go home!"

He shouted as he stamped his feet.

Essie's cat, Scaramouche,

sprang to the top of the chest of drawers, hissing.

The peddler eyed Scaramouche.
He stopped shouting,
sat down,
and put his head in his hands.

"Sometimes we decide something is no good
before we have given it a chance," Essie said.

The peddler replied, "I don't understand."

"Perhaps the monkeys will go home,
perhaps they will not.
Are they doing anything wrong?"

"No," admitted the peddler.

"Sometimes what we don't want
is exactly what we need," Essie continued.

"Go home," Essie said,
"and see what comes to pass."

The peddler frowned.
"But I won't like
what will come to pass," he said.

"Nonsense," Essie replied.
"You *cannot* dislike
what hasn't happened yet.
It's just not possible."

The peddler left Essie's house.
She chuckled as she watched the monkeys
follow her friend.
Right foot, left foot.
Right foot, left foot.
All in step.

That night, after work,
the peddler sat in his backyard
making caps.

The monkeys were busy, too.
Some were scratching their bellies.
Some were combing their hair.
Some were eating their supper.
And all were looking at him.

The peddler threaded a needle.
Then he reached for a piece of cloth.
He pulled the needle through the cloth
in and out, out and around.
He skillfully made a cap.

The peddler placed the cap in the trunk by his bench.
Then he looked up at the monkeys.
"I watch you and you watch me," he said.
The monkeys replied,
"Tsz, tsz, tsz."

Suddenly the peddler's phone rang.

The news was sad.

A friend from another town was sick.

The peddler said he would come right away.

"Oh my," he thought.
"I have money enough to travel and help,
but no time to make caps to sell tomorrow.
I hope I am not gone too long."

After the peddler left
the monkeys waited for him
to return and make the caps.

The moon came up.
                    No peddler.
The sun came up.
                    No peddler.
The moon came up.
                    No peddler.

The monkeys eyed the needles and thread.
They gazed at the pieces of cloth.
They looked at the open trunk.
                    No caps!

They were very mindful monkeys!
So what do you think they did?

One by one, the monkeys descended from the tree.

They remembered how the peddler pulled thread through the needles. Some monkeys pulled thread through the needles.

They remembered how the peddler
pulled the needles through the cloth. Some
monkeys pulled the needles through
the cloth.

They remembered how the needles went
in and out and out and around.

And soon the trunk began to fill with caps:
gray caps, brown caps, blue caps, and
red caps.

When they had sewn every piece of cloth,
the monkeys climbed up, slowly,
into the tree.
They were very tired.
And they quickly fell asleep.

Late that night
the peddler came home.
He was very tired, too.
But his friend was much better,
and that was important.

The peddler was worried.

He had no money left.
And it was too late
to make caps
to sell tomorrow.

He went outside to sit and think.
And what do you think he saw?

He looked to the right.
Caps!
He looked to the left.
Caps!
He looked behind him.
Caps!
He looked beside the tree.
More caps!

Gray caps, brown caps, blue caps, red caps.

"I don't remember making these caps,"
the peddler thought to himself.
"I must have forgotten.
But surely I did not make so many."

The peddler looked into the tree.
The monkeys seemed exhausted.
They were drooped over the branches
like old clothes.
Some were even snoring!

The peddler scratched his head
and wondered.

He looked up again.
A piece of red thread
was hanging from a monkey's foot.

"Hmm," he said to himself
as he began to pick up the caps.

Next morning when the peddler left for work,
the monkeys did not follow him.

As he began calling,
"Caps! Caps for sale!
Fifty cents a cap!"
he felt very alone,
and he wondered why.

He thought about the pile of caps
that he found last night.
He thought about the snoring monkeys
still asleep in his tree.

He thought, and then he thought some more.

Suddenly Essie's wise words
were back in the peddler's mind.
"Sometimes what we don't want is exactly what we need."

And now he knew what she was trying to tell him.

Four children approached the peddler.
"Where are your monkeys?" they asked.
"They are not my monkeys," the peddler replied.
Then he added quickly,
"But they are my friends."

That night,
when the peddler came home,
he had with him
a big bunch of bananas.

About the Title: *Caps for Sale and the Mindful Monkeys*

Most dictionaries describe the word "mindful" as "being aware of something that may be important," "to observe, to notice."

Throughout all the Caps for Sale books, the monkeys are noticing what is happening just as it is happening. They focus on the world right around them.

Because they are being mindful, they do not think about yesterday or tomorrow, and this gives them an amazing ability to pay close attention.

In this story, the monkeys' mindfulness really helps out. Because they watch the peddler intently, they learn to do something very well and come to the aid of their new friend.

Essie

About the New Characters

In homage to Esphyr Slobodkina, Sayer presents "Essie," a metaphor of Slobodkina (age 86–94), who was a celebrated author, prolific artist, and writer who lived and worked with enthusiastic energy well into her nineties.

The illustration of "Essie," drawn by Esphyr Slobodkina for her children's book entitled *Billy, the Condominium Cat*, loosely depicts a composite character of Slobodkina and her sister Tamara (age 78–86) when they resided in Florida.

During the years Slobodkina and Sayer lived and worked together, each night Sayer journaled "daily notes" of their activities, printed a copy with the heading "ES," and left it on Slobodkina's bedroom desk for her to find upon waking. Thinking back on the hundreds of pages labeled "ES" that the two women would review and discuss each morning, Sayer chose the name "Essie" based on personal memories of Slobodkina as a friend, business associate, and mentor.

"It's good fun to have been able to bring my great friend Esphyr into the stories, interacting with her beloved peddler. I think of 'Essie' (a few age lines were added to Slobodkina's orginal drawing) as my tribute to Esphyr, who constantly inspired people to be productive at every age.

"Additionally, in recognition of Slobodkina's contribution to American art, an image of a well-known Slobodkina painting will always be featured on her easel."

In *Caps for Sale and the Mindful Monkeys*, an abstract entitled "Pot Bellied Stove" (c. 1936–37) is featured. Considered one of Slobodkina's most important works, it is part of the permanent collection of the Metropolitan Museum of Art in New York.

Ann Marie Mulhearn Sayer monkeying around at the Slobodkina Foundation, 2002

Scaramouche

Scaramouche was the name of Slobodkina's real-life cat. Over the years she illustrated him many times.

Scaramouche appeared most notably in *Billy, the Condominium Cat*.

The name Scaramouche comes from an Italian comedy in which the character Scaramouche is both boastful and cowardly.

Spotty

Spotty the dog appears in two Slobodkina children's books: *Spots, Alias Prince* (c. 1987) and *Jack and Jim* (c. 1961).

The Children

The children who appear at the end of the story were selected from four different Slobodkina books. They will all have adventures with the peddler and the sixteen monkeys in future stories.

Jack is a character from the story *Jack and Jim* (c. 1961).

Billie is a character from the story *Billy, the Condominium Cat* (c. 1980).

Rose Petal is a character from the story *The Flame, the Breeze, and the Shadow* (c. 1969).

Aiesha is a character from the story *Behind the Dark Window Shade* (c. 1958).

"I believe that the formative years of childhood are relatively brief but very important segments of a person's life. The parents, the teachers, the librarians, and, yes, the writers and illustrators of children's books must take their responsibility most seriously, for the images, the verbal patterns, and the patterns of behavior they present to children in these lighthearted confections are likely to influence them for the rest of their lives. These aesthetic impressions, just like the moral teachings of early childhood, remain indelible. They will, most likely, be the bedrock upon which (or in opposition to which) a person's spiritual existence, consciously or unconsciously, will be based." —E. S.

Esphyr Slobodkina engaging children, 1978